Plan B

CHARNAN Simon

SURVIVING SOUTHSIDE

Plan B

Charnan Simon

MINNEAPOLIS

Darby Creek
A division of Lerner Publishing Group, Inc.
241 First Avenue North
Minneapolis, MN 55401 U.S.A.

Website address: www.lernerbooks.com

The images in this book are used with the permission of:
© Todd Strand/Independent Picture Service, (main image) front
cover; © iStockphoto.com/Jill Fromer, (banner background) front
cover and throughout interior; © iStockphoto.com/Naphtalina,
(brick wall background) front cover and throughout interior.

Library of Congress Cataloging-in-Publication Data

Simon, Charnan.
        Plan B / Charnan Simon.
            p.   cm. — (Surviving Southside)
        ISBN: 978-0-7613-6149-7 (lib. bdg. : alk. paper)
        [1. Pregnancy—Fiction. 2. High schools—Fiction.
    3. Schools—Fiction.] I. Title.
    PZ7.S6035Pl 2011
    [Fic]—dc22   2010023819

Manufactured in the United States of America
1 – BP – 12/31/10

FOR ARiEL,
who's TAught
ME PRACTICALLY
EVERYThing
I KNOW
—C.S.

CHAPTER 1

"Okay," I announced. "Ten reasons why today is a good day."

Cate looked at me around her locker door and groaned. "Not again!"

"Not again what?" Trez asked as she came up to us. Trez and Cate's lockers are on either side of mine.

Cate shook her head. "Just Lucy," she said. "Ms. OCD has another list going. On Friday afternoon!"

Trez laughed, but I didn't care. So what if I like lists? Nobody could ruin my mood.

"You're so right," I told Cate. "It's Friday afternoon. That's reason number one: no school for a whole weekend."

I counted off the other reasons on my fingers. "No math homework. I got an A on my Spanish test. The cafeteria had enchiladas for lunch. I traded work with Janie so I could go to Luke's baseball game tonight." I paused.

Trez pounced. "That's only five reasons, Lucy. You said you had ten."

I opened my mouth to continue. Then I saw Luke coming down the hall. He smiled at me and walked faster. I smiled back. I forgot about my list. Luke can do that. He can make me forget almost anything—except him.

Now it was Trez who groaned. "Of course!" she exclaimed. "Reasons six, seven, eight, nine, and ten are Luke! How stupid of me!" But she grinned as she said it. Trez and Cate know how I feel about Luke.

"Hello, ladies," Luke said. "How's life treating you this excellent afternoon?"

"Oh, we're fine," Trez said. "Maybe not as fine as Lucy, but fine enough."

Trez and Cate got busy digging books and backpacks out of their lockers. They're good friends that way.

"Hey," I said to Luke.

"Hey, yourself." He reached over and tucked a strand of hair behind my ear. He gave me a quick, light kiss. Then he put both hands on my shoulders and leaned in for a longer one.

I sighed. Luke and I have been going out for six months, two weeks, and four days. Since last fall, the beginning of my junior year and his senior year. I still get butterflies in my stomach just thinking about him.

"You'll be at the game tonight?" he asked.

I nodded. "Janie's working for me at the dance studio. I'm taking her shift tomorrow afternoon." I work at All That Jazz, a dance studio, after school and on weekends. It's how I pay for my dance lessons. And it beats babysitting, which is how I used to earn my spending money.

Luke kissed me again. "'Til later, then," he promised. "Coach wants us to watch the first half of the JV game this afternoon. Then I'm going home to grab a bite to eat. Do you want a ride to the game?"

I shook my head. "That's cool. Cate's picking me up." Luke has to get to the baseball field early with the rest of varsity. I used to go watch him warm up. But it made for a really long evening. I'd rather spend my time being with Luke, instead of just watching him.

"But I'd take a ride home," I added. I wrapped my arms around Luke's neck. This time I was the one doing the kissing. "If you're not too tired, that is."

"Mmmmm." Luke nuzzled my ear. "I think I can summon up the strength."

I felt a tap on my shoulder. "Break it up, kids." Principal Nuñez was doing her usual afternoon patrol of the hallways. She spoke briskly, but she sounded friendly enough. Mrs. Nuñez is okay, for a principal.

Now she smiled at Luke. "I'm looking forward to the game tonight," she said. "The West High Bobcats are a tough team."

"We can handle them," Luke said confidently. He had every reason to sound confident. If the Southside Titans kept playing the way they had been, they were headed to a state championship. As the team's best hitter and star center fielder, Luke was a big part of the team's success.

"I'm sure you can," Mrs. Nuñez said. "Especially if you save some of your energy for ball-playing." She headed down the hallway toward her office.

Cate and Trez had heard everything. "Yeah, Luke," Cate said, nudging him. "Save some of your energy for ball-playing."

Luke grinned. "Plenty more where that came from," he said. He gave me another quick kiss. "See you tonight!"

Cate, Trez, and I walked to the parking lot. Cate's the only one of us who has her own car. We made plans while she drove Trez and me home.

"I'll pick you up at seven," Cate said to me. "Unless you want to go out for a burger first?"

"Can't." I shook my head. "No money. Anyhow, I told Mom I'd have dinner with her tonight."

"How about you, Trez?" Cate persisted. "Do you want to grab a bite before the game?"

Trez shook her head too. "I'm going with Lonzo," she said. "We'll probably just eat something at the game."

I raised my eyebrows. "You and Lonzo are back on?" I asked. "When did this happen?"

"We've never exactly been off," Trez said. "We were just sort of taking a break." She sighed. "I mean, I like Lonzo and everything. But having a boyfriend is so much work!"

I smiled to myself. I didn't think having a boyfriend was work at all. Not Luke.

"Oh, stop it!" wailed Cate. "Not fair. I'd take a little of that work! I haven't even been on a date since Homecoming. And that was just Ricky Stanton!"

Trez and I exchanged glances. Cate's lack of a boyfriend was a familiar topic of conversation. We spent the rest of the ride trying to cheer her up.

CHAPTER 2

I 'm home, Mom!" I called out as I let myself in the front door of our apartment. I dumped my backpack on the floor.

"Hey, sweetie," she called back. "I'm in the kitchen. How was school?"

Mom asks me this every day. Once I added it up. I'm in eleventh grade. I've been in school twelve years, if you count kindergarten. (And I do. Kindergarten was my favorite grade.

Coloring and recess and snack time—it doesn't get any better than that.) For each of those twelve years I've gone to school maybe 180 days. If you do the math, that makes over two thousand days. You'd think Mom would get tired of asking the same question so many times.

I don't really mind. Unlike some of my friends, I get along with my mom. I actually *like* talking to her. Maybe it's because she's pretty young for a mother. She had me when she was seventeen, my age. She remembers what it's like to be a kid.

Or maybe we get along because it's always been just the two of us. I don't have a father. I mean, I *have* a father, like everyone does. His name is Jake Doherty. He was eighteen when Mom had me. He stuck around exactly six weeks after I was born. Then he tucked $250 in my diaper bag and left us. Today Jake lives in Tulsa, Oklahoma. Or at least he did the last time we heard from him. He sends Mom money when he's working, and I've gotten a few birthday cards from him over the years, but that's pretty much it.

"Your dad wasn't a bad guy" is the most Mom usually says about Jake. "He just wasn't ready to be a father."

I walked into the kitchen. Mom was standing at the counter, slicing tomatoes. "I thought we'd eat picnic-style tonight," she said. "BLTs and fruit salad and cupcakes. You can cut up the fruit."

"You made cupcakes?" I said. "That's so cute!" I peeked at the foil-covered tray. "You even put on sprinkles!"

Mom looked a little sheepish. "I was tired of reading about anatomy," she said. "Cupcakes seemed like the best study break."

Mom's studying to be a medical transcriptionist. That's someone who listens to dictations by doctors and then uses a computer to write up reports. I'm really proud of her. She had a bunch of different jobs while I was growing up. When I was really little, she worked in a daycare center and took me with her. At night she waitressed while Mrs. Poole from downstairs watched me. When I started elementary school, she got a job in the school cafeteria. By the time I went to middle school, she'd gotten her GED. She started working in offices and doing telemarketing from our apartment. She always tried to be home when I got home from school. "There's nothing wrong with latchkey kids," she'd say. "I just like to be here when you walk through that door."

For the past couple of years, Mom's been a receptionist in my pediatrician's office. But not too long ago, Dr. Allen started asking her to transcribe some letters and reports. Mom turned out to be really good at it. Dr. Allen encouraged her to get her certification.

"I'll have to go to school at night," Mom had told me. "But you're old enough to be home alone. And it'll mean a lot more money. We might even save enough for a down payment on a house!"

Buying our own house has always been Mom's dream. Personally, I like our apartment just fine. And in two years I'll be off to college. But I like seeing Mom so excited about her future. She's worked really hard all her life.

She hasn't had help from anyone. If she wants to buy a house, she should be able to!

We took our sandwiches and fruit out to the tiny balcony off the kitchen. Mom stretched and kicked off her sandals. "It feels good to sit down," she said. "This has been a rough week!"

"You sure you don't want to come to Luke's game?" I asked. Mom likes baseball. She doesn't sit with me or anything, but sometimes she goes for fun.

"Not a chance!" she said. "I'm going to finish my anatomy review. Then I'm curling up in bed with the remote. I have a full day at Dr. Allen's tomorrow. I'm knocking off early tonight."

"I'll be quiet when I come in," I promised. "I don't think it'll be late. Luke's got an out-of-town game tomorrow afternoon, so he'll need to turn in early tonight too."

"I love these training season rules," Mom said, yawning. She stretched again. "Tell Luke I said good luck tonight. Now bring me my cupcake before I fall asleep!"

CHAPTER 3

It was a perfect night for a baseball game. The sun was just starting to set in a cloudless sky. The air was warm and balmy. Cate and I made our way to our favorite seats along the first-base line.

I waved to Trez and Lonzo. They were sharing a hot dog and a bag of popcorn. Trez looked happy enough. Having a boyfriend didn't seem like hard work for her tonight.

Cate waved too. Then she sighed. "You two are so lucky," she said. She plopped herself down on the bleachers. "I've been thinking. Maybe it's not me. Maybe it's just that high-school boys are so juvenile. What if I took some classes at Houston Community College this summer? I bet I'd meet a guy there!"

"What are you going to take?" I teased. "Boyfriend 101? Summer School Sex?"

Cate threw a peanut shell at me. "You laugh, but you just wait. I'll be the only girl in Engineering or Auto Mechanics. All the guys will be falling over me. Or how about this—I could take a paramedics course. Then I could hang out with all those future firemen!"

I focused on the field once the game started. I love to watch Luke play baseball. Luke's a natural athlete. He's fast on his feet and has a really strong throwing arm. He makes it all look easy.

Plus he's got a great butt.

Southside won the game 7-4. Luke had three hits—a single, a double, and a two-run homer. When he caught the last out at the top of the seventh, he looked for me in the bleachers. I stood up and waved. As he jogged back to the dugout, he tossed me the ball. It's one of our rituals. I have a stash of last-out balls from Luke's games. Mom's always threatening to toss them, but I won't let her.

I hung around with Cate until Luke came out of the showers. Luke's mom and dad were there too. It was their night to work at the booster club concession stand. I could have gone over to say hi, but I just sort of waved. They were busy closing up the stand. Also, I'm still not sure Mr. and Mrs. Gilman really like me.

When Luke came out, Coach Martin was with him. They went over to talk to Luke's parents. Something more than the game was going on. Luke's mom gave him a big hug. His dad shook Coach Martin's hand and clapped Luke on the back.

"Wonder what that's all about?" Cate asked.

"Me too," I said. "I'll let you know at dance tomorrow."

Cate took off, and Luke came trotting over to me. "Great game!" I said, throwing my arms around him.

"Mmmmm," he said, hugging back. "You smell good." He kissed me. "And you taste even better!" he whispered in my ear.

"So," I said as we started toward his car, fingers intertwined, "what's going on with Coach and your parents?"

"The scout from Austin was here again," Luke said. He sounded excited. "Coach talked to him after the game."

"Luke! That's awesome!" Luke's already been accepted at the University of Texas at Austin for next year. Now he's waiting to hear about a baseball scholarship. He's got a good chance for a full ride. "What did he say?"

"Don't know. Coach just said he was here and wants to meet me. Soon. He'll call Coach and my dad to set something up."

We got in the car and sat for a minute. This really was good news. Luke and I have our futures all planned. One time I even wrote it out, in list form. First: Luke wins a baseball scholarship to UT, where he majors in physical education. Second: I graduate in the top ten percent of my class at Southside so I can get a scholarship to study Spanish at UT next year. Third: we have a wonderful time in college. Fourth: we graduate and find jobs at the same high school—Luke as the athletic director and me as a Spanish teacher. Fifth: we get married and live happily ever after.

Luke grinned. He knew what I was thinking. "Everything okay, Lucy? You got your list all in order?"

I laughed. "But what if I can't get a scholarship? I don't think my mom can afford to send me to college."

Luke gave me another hug. "Are you kidding? You're the smartest girl I know, Lucy. You'll get a scholarship!"

I cuddled into Luke's arms. "What if I'm not as smart you think?"

"Not likely! Tell me again what you got on your Spanish test today . . . ?"

I punched him on the shoulder. Luke already knew I got 100.

Luke kissed my nose. "It's going to happen, Lucy," he said confidently. "Just like we planned."

We stopped talking and got serious about kissing. I love kissing Luke. I love everything about the way he feels and tastes and smells. When I'm kissing Luke, I never want to stop.

"*¿Te gusta?*" he whispered, stroking my hair. Luke may not know as much Spanish as I do. But he knows enough.

"*Sí,*" I whispered back. "*Me gusta. Me gusta mucho!*"

CHAPTER 4

Mom dropped me off at the dance studio early Saturday morning. "You're sure you've got a ride home?" she asked. "I'm supposed to meet my study group at the library right after work. But I could swing by and take you home first."

I shook my head. "Luke's picking me up after his game. We'll probably go out for something to eat. Or we might just rent a movie and stay home tonight."

"Okay then." Mom looked me in the eye and said the other thing she always says. "Have fun, be smart, stay safe." Then she added, "And eat the rest of those cupcakes!"

I got out of the car and waved. "Good luck with studying!"

Saturdays are always busy at the dance studio. The little-kid classes are in the morning. Things are pretty noisy and chaotic. I check kids in and field questions and answer the phone. Today I was also updating our website. We've just set the date for our spring show, and I had to put all the performance information online. *Plus* collect costume fees and get a head count for tickets.

"Six tickets please, Lucy," said Mrs. Murphy. Mrs. Murphy is one of my favorite moms. She and her three-year-old daughter Tierney take our Saturday morning Dancin' Tots class. Usually she brings her four-month-old, TJ, and lets him watch from his infant seat.

"Six tickets," I said, checking them off. "It's a good thing you're ordering early. We might sell out this year!"

"Tierney's grandparents would never forgive me if I didn't get their tickets," Mrs. Murphy said. "Neither would Tierney, for that matter."

A lot of little kids can be whiny. TJ and Tierney are just cute. TJ crowed and smiled when he saw me. Tierney wanted to show me her new purple underpants. Mrs. Murphy rolled her eyes, but I told Tierney I thought they were beautiful.

The morning went by quickly. By one, the little kids had pretty much cleared out. Now it was my turn.

I love dancing. Cate, Trez, and I are on Southside's dance team and take classes together at All That Jazz. When the music's playing and I'm moving across the floor, I feel like my best self. It's not like I want to be a professional dancer or anything. I know I'm not good enough. Cate's better than I am, for instance. She takes ballet as well as jazz.

She has a better body, better technique. But I think I love dancing more than Cate does.

There's a poster on the studio wall. It has a quote by a dancer named Agnes de Mille. She said, "To dance is to be out of yourself. Larger, more beautiful, more powerful." That poster sums up exactly how I feel when I dance.

Of course, I also feel hot, sweaty, and sometimes sore. Our teacher, Toni, doesn't mess around in class. We really have to work. Especially now, with the show only a few months away. We've just started learning our new routine. It's a hard one.

By the time class ended, Cate and Trez and I were dripping. We collapsed on the floor of the changing room.

"Too much!" Trez groaned, massaging her calves. "I didn't get enough sleep for this much effort!"

"Ooooh," Cate said, fanning herself. "Good time with Lonzo last night?"

Trez rolled over on her back. "It's always a good time with Lonzo," she said. "Sometimes

I think we should just have sex and get it over with."

"Trez!" I said. I was sort of shocked. "Are you serious? I didn't know that you and Lonzo—that you *did* that kind of stuff."

"Oh, come on, Lucy." Trez sounded impatient. "Don't tell me that you and Luke *don't* do 'that kind of stuff.'"

"We do," I said slowly. "But it's different . . ." My voice trailed off.

"Different how?" Trez asked. "You kiss, you fumble around in the dark, you feel his hands where they really shouldn't be, you think 'maybe tonight,' you decide you'd rather have ice cream instead."

I couldn't help laughing. Trez can be funny when she wants to.

"Is that how it is with you and Luke?" Cate asked me. "The fumbling, the ice cream?"

I laughed again. "It *is* different for me and Luke," I said. "For one thing, I'd never rather have ice cream."

Trez snorted.

But then I got serious. "I wouldn't have sex just to get it over with," I said honestly. "I'd have sex with Luke because I love him."

I was quiet for a minute, remembering Luke. "I'd be making love," I said finally. "And that's different."

CHAPTER 5

I was tired and hungry by the time Luke picked me up. "Get me out of here!" I exclaimed as I hopped in the car.

We drove around for a while, talking about our days, deciding what to do. I told Luke about our new dance routine. He told me about his ball game. Southside won again; Luke's seventh-inning double scored the winning run.

I thought that deserved a congratulatory kiss at the next red light.

"So," Luke said, kissing back, "what do you want to eat?"

I kissed him again. "You taste pretty good."

He reached over and squeezed my knee. His hand wandered, and I batted it away. "Oh, no," he said. "You tease, I squeeze."

"The light's green," I said. "Pay attention to your driving, sir."

He gave my leg another squeeze and then put his hand back on the steering wheel. "You want to go to a movie?" he asked.

I thought about it. "Not really," I said truthfully. "I'm tired. I'd rather just get some takeout and watch something at home. Mom's at the library, so we could have the apartment to ourselves."

I don't know why I thought picking out a DVD would be easier than choosing a movie at the theater. Luke and I are pretty predictable. He likes sports movies and action films. I like something with a good story.

"A good love story, you mean," he said. "A chick flick. Ninety minutes of sensitivity and heartbreak."

"It's better than ninety minutes of blood and gore," I countered.

In the end we agreed on *Love & Basketball*. It has something for both of us—sports and a good story and great characters. And, let's be honest—some pretty hot sex scenes. It's sort of the perfect date movie. With *Love & Basketball* and a mountain of food from Taco Shack, Luke and I were set for the night.

"Any more news about the scout from Austin?" I asked as I took the last bite of my quesadilla.

Luke had already finished his tacos and refried beans. He was moving on to Mom's cupcakes.

"Not yet," he said. "Coach thinks he's waiting to see if I make All-State."

"Of course you'll make All-State!" I said. "You did last year! You're the best center fielder in the league!"

But Luke shook his head. "I don't know, Lucy. Carlos Moreno at Uniondale is pretty good. He's only a junior, but he's having a really good year."

I don't like to see Luke look discouraged. It was time for a change of scene. I went over to the couch. I patted the cushion next to me.

"Come on," I said. "Put on the movie and let's chill."

For a while Luke and I just snuggled. By the time the movie got to the steamy scene after the dance, we weren't really watching anymore. We were too busy kissing.

"Mmmm," I murmured. I shifted on the couch. Luke was stretched out half next to me, half on top of me. I wrapped my arms tighter around his neck. Luke pressed against me, kissing me hard.

I closed my eyes and kissed back. I remembered what I'd said to Trez and Cate at the dance studio. "I wouldn't have sex just to get it over with," I'd told my friends. "I'd have sex because I love Luke."

Is this the night? I wondered. *Are we going to have sex tonight?* Part of me was tingly with anticipation. I love kissing Luke. And I was pretty sure I'd love doing other things with Luke too.

But another part of me was tingly with nervousness. *What if Mom came back early? What if she caught us having sex on the couch? What about staying safe? I'm not on birth control. Does Luke have a condom? Would I know how to ask him to use it? Would he know how?*

I opened my eyes. "Luke," I whispered.

Luke pushed himself up on one arm. He traced my mouth with his finger. He kissed me on my eyelids and my nose.

I shifted on the couch again, this time to sit up. "It's getting late," I said. "Mom's going to be home soon."

Luke just sighed and reached for me again. But I scooted down to the other end of the couch. "Up," I commanded.

"You're no fun," he grumbled. But he sat up. We ate more cupcakes. We finished the movie. By the time Mom walked in, we were arguing about whether Monica or Quincy was the better basketball player.

CHAPTER 6

I didn't see much of Luke for the next couple of days. Sunday is sort of a family day. Mom and I sleep in as late as we want. We eat cinnamon rolls for breakfast and read the Sunday paper. Well, Mom reads the paper. I look at the comics. In the afternoon Mom does the crossword while I do homework. We make out a grocery list and go to the farmers' market. If it's nice, we take a bike ride. If the apartment's a mess, we blast up the CD player and clean. I usually text Luke while I study. But that's about it.

On Monday, I had a noon dance-club meeting, so I couldn't see Luke at lunch. Then he had an away game after school. The varsity bus left right after seventh period. Luke called me when he got home, but it was too late to get together.

"How about tomorrow night?" he asked. "Can we do something after your dance class? It's been forever since we've gotten together!"

I felt the same way. "Come over around eight," I said. "Mom has class, so Cate's giving me a ride home from dance."

Tuesdays are always busy. I work at the studio right after school. Cate gives me a ride and takes her Ballet IV class while I work. She goes home for dinner while I eat whatever I've brought from home. Then Cate, Trez, and I have jazz class at 6:30.

Mom's busy too. She goes straight to class from work. Her Tuesday class doesn't get out until nine.

"I'll be a little late tonight," Mom said when she dropped me off at school. "Some of us are going out for wine and dessert after class. We're celebrating making it through midterms!"

"Have fun," I said. Usually I was the one staying out late. I couldn't help adding, "Be smart. Stay safe!"

Mom made a face. "After this semester, things will slow down—promise!"

The day went fast. School was okay. Work was slow. Cate, Trez, and I were just putting on our jazz shoes when Luke burst into the studio a little before 6:30.

"Luke!" I said, surprised. "What are you doing here?"

He practically lifted me off the bench. "I made All-State!" he said. "They just posted the list—I'm on the A team! Coach says the Austin scout has already called about setting up our meeting!"

I gave a little squeal. I couldn't help it. "Luke! That's so great!"

He spun me around with a kiss. "I know you've got class," he said. "I won't stay. But I had to tell you! See you at eight!"

Cate and Trez crowded around after Luke left.

"That's awesome," Cate said. "I bet he gets a scholarship for sure now!"

Trez was more matter-of-fact. "You didn't really think he *wouldn't* make All-State, did you?" she asked. "But the thing with the Austin scout is pretty exciting!"

Toni stuck her head past the changing room door. "Ladies!" she said sharply. "Are you dancing or are you talking? Class starts *now*!"

I couldn't help thinking about Luke all through class. By the time Cate dropped me off at the apartment, I had our night all planned, in list form.

"First: I'll order Zeek's Kitchen Sink pizza," I ticked off on my fingers. "Then I'll light candles. I'll use placemats and real napkins. I'll put my favorite playlist on my iPod. Everything's going to be special tonight."

Cate nodded approvingly. "I wish I could do that for someone!"

Luke was still excited when he came over. "Just talked to the scout," he said. "Dad and I are driving to Austin a week from Saturday. We're getting a tour of the university and meeting the whole coaching staff. I might even warm up with the team!"

I poured soda into Mom's wine glasses while Luke talked. It was a celebration, wasn't it? Then I had a thought: *celebrations call for more than just soda.* I pulled up a chair and checked the cabinet over the refrigerator.

Yes! There was a bottle of vodka. Mom doesn't drink much. But sometimes she likes a Bloody Mary on Sunday mornings or a vodka tonic on hot summer afternoons.

I've tasted both of those drinks. I don't like either. But I know from parties that vodka tastes okay if you mix it with juice.

I poured the soda down the sink and put some vodka in our glasses. Then I filled them up with orange juice.

"Cheers!" I toasted Luke. "To you! To us!"

Luke looked surprised. Then he grinned. "To us!"

We took our wine glasses to the couch. Luke talked about visiting Austin. He talked about what it would be like to live in a dorm. He talked about fraternities and traveling with the university baseball team. As he got more and more excited, I got more and more quiet.

Finally he noticed. "What's wrong, Lucy?" he asked. "This is what we want!"

"I know it is," I said. "It's just—" I took a swallow of my orange juice and tried again. "It's just that I've never really thought about it before! About you being there, I mean, and me being here."

I took another swallow. It tasted a little bitter, but the warm buzz was comforting. "What if you forget me? I'll still just be in high school! You'll have all those college girls around you. Sorority girls. Cheerleaders! They might live right next to you! And they'll all like your butt too!" I ended in a wail.

Luke took me in his arms. "Lucy, Lucy," he murmured in my ear, "this is crazy talk! I could never forget you! I won't be looking at cheerleaders! I've got you! When you come to visit, you'll stay right in my room, not next door!"

Luke was kissing me as he talked. He pressed me against the couch cushions. He kissed my face, my shoulders, my neck. His lips were warm against my body. I thought about cheerleaders and kissed back. I arched up against him. I let my hands go places they'd never gone before.

Luke's breath got raggedy. He put his hands under my shirt and undid my bra. I let him. I felt warm and melty.

I love Luke. I don't ever want him to forget me.

When Luke unzipped my jeans, I didn't tell him to stop.

CHAPTER 7

Having sex with Luke was everything and nothing like what I expected. We were a little shy around each other as we got dressed. "Maybe we should eat the pizza," I said.

Luke looked sort of relieved. We put away the vodka bottle and filled our wine glasses with soda. We ate the cold pizza. We started talking and laughing again. Not about what we'd just done. Just about normal stuff. But everything felt different.

Luke didn't stay late. He gave me a long, lingering kiss when he left. "You were amazing tonight, Lucy," he said softly.

I was sure Mom would notice something different about me the next morning. But she just chatted about her class and her night out. She was pleased when I told her about Luke and All-State.

"Be sure to tell Luke congratulations for me," she said. "I'll keep my fingers crossed for his scholarship!"

Cate and Trez didn't seem to notice anything different either. Only Luke knew. When he came to my locker after school, he smiled meaningfully. His kiss was more urgent than usual, more probing.

"Hey," he said softly, "I thought about you all night. When can I see you again?"

I felt tingly again. "Tonight," I said. "You can see me tonight."

Everything changed after that night. From then on, when Luke and I got together, we thought about how and where we could be alone. It wasn't enough just to hold hands and kiss anymore. Once you've gone all the way, nothing else is good enough. It wasn't just Luke either. I wanted him as much as he wanted me.

Mostly we went to my apartment when Mom was at class. Once in a while we went to Luke's house, if both his parents were out. We started taking our time, getting to know each other's bodies. Except for sometimes. Sometimes we just got carried away. We did it hot and hurried. In the backseat of Luke's car. In the front seat of Luke's car. On our couch, like the first time.

But always after that first time, Luke used a condom.

Meanwhile, the rest of my life carried on as usual. I still went to school and work. I still made dinner with Mom. I still cheered for Luke at his baseball games and rehearsed for the spring dance show. Everything else was the same. But I was different.

I was at the dance studio when I told Cate and Trez. Part of me wanted to tell them right from the beginning. They're my best friends, after all. And sleeping with Luke is big news. But part of me wanted to keep things private, at least for a little while. Making love is special. It's just between me and Luke. What we do together isn't for gossip and girl talk. So I surprised myself when I just sort of blurted it out one Saturday when we were getting dressed after class.

"Who wants to go to the mall?" Cate asked. "It's Sidewalk Sale day."

"I do," I said without thinking. "I need to go to Bare Essentials. Luke snapped the strap off my black bra last night when we—"

I stopped. I felt my face start to turn red.

"When you *what*?" Trez demanded. "Luke snapped the strap off your black bra when you *what*?"

Cate pounced. "Lucy Anne! Have you been holding out on us? Are you and Luke doing it?"

"Shhhhh!" I said. I gathered up my dance bag and hurried them out the door. "I'll tell you in the car!"

And I did. Not everything, of course. But enough.

"That's it!" Cate exclaimed. "I'm calling Ricky Stanton. I'm tired of being the only one without a sex life!"

"I guess I'll have to sleep with Lonzo after all," Trez said gloomily. "Either that or break up with him. Once Lonzo finds out Luke's getting some, I'll never hear the end of it."

I bristled. "Lonzo's not finding out anything!" I said. "Luke's not going to tell everyone he's sleeping with me!"

Trez looked at me. "Like you're not telling everyone you're sleeping with Luke?"

"You're not everyone," I said. "You're my best friends!"

"And Lonzo's one of Luke's best friends," Trez said logically. "These things get around, Lucy. Cate and I aren't going to blab. But people start to talk." She shrugged. "But so what? Having sex is nothing to be ashamed of. Is it?"

Of course it isn't. But I was upset all the same. Making love with Luke was my own special, private business. I didn't see why the rest of the world had to know all about it.

CHAPTER 8

As it turned out, I didn't have to worry. If Lonzo knew that Luke and I were having sex, he didn't say anything. And I was too happy to care all that much.

Luke came back from his visit to Austin all pumped up. He wouldn't find out about the scholarship for a while. But all the signs looked good.

"You'll love Austin," he told me. "It's completely different from Houston. And the campus is great!"

He even brought me a present. An orange Texas Longhorns T-shirt. He got one for himself, too, but mine is the fitted, girl's version. I love wearing it.

I had good news of my own. "Toni's giving me and Cate solos in the spring show," I told Luke. "I knew Cate would get one. But Toni choreographed a solo for me too!"

The solo meant extra rehearsal times. I was busier than ever. So I was especially bummed out when I felt a flu bug coming on.

Mom noticed it first when I didn't make it into the kitchen until way past noon one Sunday.

"I could sleep all day," I moaned. "I am soooo tired." I poured a glass of orange juice, then put it back. "And my stomach doesn't feel so hot either."

Mom came over and felt my forehead. "I hope I didn't bring home that tummy bug that's going around," she said. "We've been swamped with sick kids at the office."

Mom's always worrying that she'll give me some germ from Dr. Allen's office.

"I doubt it," I told her. "Everyone at school is sick too. Spring fever. Only not the good kind."

Mom made me lie down on the couch. She brought me ginger ale and toast and the comics, just like I was a little kid again. "To help you feel better," she said.

It almost made me feel worse. I'd been feeling bad about not telling Mom about me and Luke. I'm not used to keeping secrets from her. I'm not sure why I didn't just tell her. It's not like Mom doesn't understand about teenagers having sex.

Mom's always been very up-front with me. "I hope you'll wait to have sex until you're an old married lady," she told me a couple years ago. "But if you don't—be smart." She brought home all kinds of birth control and talked about how to use them. And she ended by saying, "I also hope you'll tell me if you start having sex. But if you don't want to talk to me, call Dr. Allen. She'll keep your talk confidential."

Now it felt almost like a lie, not telling Mom about me and Luke. But I just wasn't ready. Maybe after I feel better, I told myself.

The bug was tough to shake. "Maybe I have mono," I told Trez. "All I want to do is sleep!"

Trez shook her head. "You don't have a sore throat," she said. "It's probably not mono. You're just not getting enough rest." She grinned. "Luke's wearing you out, girl!"

Once I had a dizzy spell while I was rehearsing my solo. One minute I was arched back in a jazz layout. The next minute, my head was spinning and I was grabbing at the barre for support.

Toni was beside me in a second. "Lie down," she said sharply. "Stay there. Breathe." She brought me a drink of water and had me sit up, slowly. She rocked back on her heels and studied me.

"It's not like you to faint, Lucy. Are you dieting?" she asked bluntly. "You know how I feel about dieting!"

Did I ever. Toni's always warning us about dancers and eating disorders. If she thinks one of her dancers has a problem with food, she doesn't hesitate. She calls parents and sets up doctor appointments.

I shook my head. "It's just a flu bug," I said. "I thought I was over it." When Toni still looked concerned, I managed a smile. "You know me, Toni. I like my carbs too much to diet!"

Toni laughed then and rubbed my shoulders. "Go home," she said. "Get better. We'll set up another rehearsal next week."

But I didn't feel better the next week. I started feeling really nauseous. I could just look at food and get queasy. Smells too. I couldn't stand the smell of cafeteria enchiladas, and they used to be my favorite. I was crampy and bloated.

Then it hit me. *My period*, I thought. *I'm getting my period! With all the stress and excitement, my period's late. A late period can make anyone feel crummy. Especially if it comes right on top of a flu bug.*

The relief I felt was almost immediately replaced with panic.

My period was late.

CHAPTER 9

I couldn't sleep that night. Every time I closed my eyes, I saw one of those stock market ticker-tape things, like in the movie we watched in Econ. Only instead of numbers, it was words scrolling past my closed eyelids.

My period's late my period's late my period's late.

I tried to argue with myself. My period's never been what you'd call really regular. I couldn't remember exactly when I had it last.

So maybe it wasn't surprising that I didn't notice it was late this month. I'd been late lots of other times.

Except I wasn't having sex all those other times.

But still. If you didn't count the first time, Luke and I had always used condoms. And they'd never broken either.

Nobody gets pregnant the first time they have sex.

Pregnant.

Just thinking the word made me break out in a sweat.

Of course people get pregnant the first time they have sex. Only a moron doesn't know that.

I'm a moron. A probably pregnant moron.

Finally my alarm went off. I got out of bed and took a long, hot shower. I spent extra time on my hair and makeup. I wanted to look as nonpregnant as possible.

I didn't do anything except worry for a couple of days. *If it's my period*, I reasoned, it'll start, and *everything will be fine. If not . . .* I didn't let myself go there.

Life kept going on as usual around me. Luke was headed to the playoffs, so he was always at practice or a game. I was going from school to work to rehearsal to bed. Mom and I were eating a lot of sandwiches for dinner. It seemed we were always passing each other coming and going. She kept apologizing for her crazy schedule. But I was relieved she wasn't around to pay more attention to me.

By Thursday I couldn't stand it anymore. My period still hadn't come. And now my breasts were starting to feel achy. I looked up pregnancy symptoms online before I left for school. Tiredness, nausea, cramping, tender breasts—I was a textbook case.

The day crawled by. For once I was glad I had a dance club meeting at noon. I was glad Luke had to leave for his away game right after school. I couldn't talk to him about this yet. I could barely talk to him about anything. I watched the team bus roll away with a feeling of relief.

Cate and Trez were waiting for me in the parking lot.

"Hurry up, Lucy," Cate called. She jingled her car keys impatiently. "We'll be late for rehearsal."

I made a snap decision. "I can't go to rehearsal," I said. "I need to go to the drugstore. I need you to come with me."

Trez looked concerned. "You're still really that sick?" she asked. "Maybe you should see a doctor."

I felt a little hysterical. "I'm not sick," I said. "I'm pregnant."

There was a stunned silence.

". . . I think."

Trez was the first to recover. "Get in the car, Lucy," she said firmly. "You can tell us on the way."

There really wasn't much to tell. "My period's late," I said flatly. "I'm tired. I have morning sickness. I need a pregnancy test."

I wouldn't let Cate go to our neighborhood drugstore. "What if I meet someone I know? Go downtown. Or someplace else. Anyplace but here."

Cate talked excitedly as she drove. "My cousin in Galveston had a baby last year. It's the cutest little girl. My uncle was furious. But my aunt said there are worse things in the world than raising your sixteen-year-old daughter's baby."

"Shut up, Cate," Trez said. She patted my shoulder. Then she blurted out, "But how could you let this happen, Lucy?"

What could I say? "Just stupid, I guess."

Trez looked sorry she'd opened her mouth.

I had no idea there were so many home pregnancy tests. I picked the kind that spelled the words right out: "pregnant" or "not pregnant." I didn't want to make things any more confusing than they had to be.

Trez read the directions as we drove back to my apartment. "It says results are most accurate if the test is done first thing in the morning. That's when the pregnant hormones in your pee are strongest."

"I'm not waiting 'til tomorrow morning," I said.

I didn't need to. My pregnant pee was plenty strong right now. I didn't even have to wait the full five minutes before the little strip flashed "pregnant."

Cate squealed. "Lucy! You're pregnant! We can have a baby shower, like we did for my cousin!"

Trez told Cate to shut up again. She tried to reassure me. "It could be a false positive. It says you're supposed to repeat the test twice, a week apart."

The two of them started arguing. I didn't listen. I couldn't really hear what they were saying anyhow. Now the ticker tape in my brain had a loudspeaker attached.

I'M PREGNANT! I'M PREGNANT! I'M PREGNANT!

CHAPTER 10

After a while I kicked Trez and Cate out. I couldn't listen to Trez make plans to take me to Planned Parenthood. I couldn't listen to Cate talk about getting pregnant too, so we could raise our babies together.

All I wanted was to see Luke.

And yet—I was terrified to see Luke.

He called as soon as he got home from his game. I listened to him talk. Then I told him I was sleepy and had to hang up. I knew

I couldn't tell him anything this big over the phone.

"I'm already in bed," I said. That was probably a mistake.

Luke's voice got lower. "I wish I were in bed with you," he said softly. "I wish I could be in bed with you every night."

My morning sickness was in full force the next day. I ran the shower so Mom wouldn't hear me throwing up. I sucked on lemon drops all the way to school.

Luke was waiting by my locker. "Hey, you," he said, "missed you yesterday." He gave me his usual close hug, his usual lingering kiss.

"No practice today," he said. "I can give you a ride home from work."

I shook my head. "I'm not working today. Janie's taking my shift."

Luke tightened his grip. "So we can go straight to your apartment?"

This wasn't what I meant. "I sort of feel like doing something different today," I said. "It's so nice out—can we go to the park? Just sit and talk for a while?" I thought it might be easier to talk outdoors.

Luke ran his hands down my back. "How about park first, then your apartment?"

We never made it to my apartment. We went to the park and found a sunny spot near the duck pond. We spread the blanket Luke keeps in the trunk of his car. Luke pulled me down next to him.

"Come here, you," he murmured. He stroked my shoulders and started kissing.

I pushed away. "Luke," I said, "we need to talk."

And then I just told him. About the morning sickness. About being tired. About the pregnancy test.

At first he didn't get it. "What are you talking about, Lucy?"

"I'm talking about being pregnant, Luke. I'm pregnant. I'm having a baby."

Luke jumped back like he'd touched a hot flame. "A baby?" he almost shouted. "What do you mean, you're having a baby! You can't be!"

I felt suddenly tired. "I can be. I am."

Luke stood up. He walked away. He came back. "I don't get it! I always use a condom. How can you be pregnant? Are you sure it's mi—" He stopped just in time.

I felt like I'd been punched in the stomach. "Am I sure it's what, Luke? Am I sure it's yours?" Now I was the one shouting. "Who else's could it be? Who else do you think I sleep with?" I burst into tears. Everything I'd been holding in the past week came pouring out in big, gasping sobs. I thought being pregnant was the worst that could happen. I was so wrong.

Luke walked around, clenching and unclenching his fists. He cursed under his breath. Finally he sat back down. He took a deep breath. "That was a stupid thing for me to say, Lucy," he said in a low voice. "I didn't mean it. It's just—I don't—"

He stopped talking. I kept crying.

Luke put an arm around my shoulders. He gave a little squeeze. "I'm sorry," he said. "I didn't mean it. I'm really, really sorry."

Eventually I stopped crying. "It must have been that first time," I said miserably. "That's all I can think."

We sat quietly for a while, thinking. Remembering.

"What—" We both started talking at the same time.

I laughed a little, shakily. "You first."

Luke shook his head. "I was just going to ask what you're going to do," he said. He avoided my eyes. "My parents are going to kill me when they find out."

I was suddenly really scared. Scared of being pregnant. Scared of having a baby. Scared of telling my mom. Scared of losing Luke.

Luke hadn't asked what *we* were going to do. He asked what *I* was going to do.

"I don't know," I finally answered sadly. "I just don't know."

I tried to make Luke look at me. He kept his arm around me. But he wouldn't meet my eyes.

Chapter 11

Luke didn't come in when he took me home. "I'll call you," he said. "I need some time to think."

I went straight to bed. But I couldn't sleep. I just lay there, miserable. Every time my cell went off, my heart leapt. But it was never Luke. I didn't pick up the calls from Trez and Cate. I didn't answer their texts either. I couldn't talk to them right now.

I did pick up when Mom called. "Hey!" she said. "I'm glad I caught you. I'm going out after class tonight. I figured since it's Friday you'll be busy anyhow. I won't be too late."

"That's fine," I said. I tried to sound cheerful and busy. "Have fun!"

After a while I got up and made myself some toast. I munched slowly. I turned on my laptop. Even though it scared me, I Googled "teen pregnancy" and made myself read. I learned some stuff I didn't know. The normal pregnancy lasts forty weeks. You start counting from the first day of your last period.

I tried to remember when my last period was. Five weeks ago? Six? Maybe seven? *Great*, I thought. *I don't even know how pregnant I am.*

I made a list. I had three choices:

I could have the baby and raise it myself.

I could have the baby and give it up for adoption.

I could have an abortion.

The choices all sucked. I added a fourth: Pretend it never happened. Then I turned off my laptop and cried myself to sleep.

I honestly don't know how I made it through Saturday. Mom dropped me off at the dance studio as usual. I sleepwalked my way through work in the morning. I managed to pull myself together for class in the afternoon.

Trez and Cate and I didn't talk much until we were driving home.

"I told Luke," I said as soon as we were in the car.

"What did he say?" asked Cate. "Was he excited?"

"Not exactly," I said. I didn't want to go into details.

"What are you going to do, Lucy?" asked Trez. "Have you told your mom yet?"

I shook my head. "I guess I should. But she's been so busy lately, I hate to bother her . . ." My voice trailed off.

Trez was quiet for a minute. "Lucy," she said gently, "you won't be *bothering* your mom. She's going to find out sooner or later. And it's just going to be harder, the longer you wait."

"Not if I have an abortion," I said abruptly. "If I have an abortion Mom will never need to find out."

Cate looked horrified. "You wouldn't!"

I didn't know if I would or not. When we talked about stuff like abortion in Social Issues class, I always said it was a woman's right to choose. Now that I was the woman, I wasn't sure. All the choices looked hard.

"You'd still have to tell your mom," Trez said seriously. "You're under eighteen and you're not married. In Texas, that means you need a parent's written permission to get an abortion."

I felt hysterical again. "Luke and I could get married, and *then* I could have an abortion." Even I knew how stupid that sounded. "I just wish I could talk to Luke again before I tell Mom."

But that didn't happen. Luke didn't answer his phone when I called him. He didn't answer my texts either.

By the time Mom got home, I was a mess. Being scared and sad and sick isn't a good combination.

Mom looked really tired when she came in. I was afraid to hit her with my news right then. But suddenly I needed to talk. I needed my mom to hug me and tell me everything would be all right.

That didn't happen either.

I blurted out the story of how Luke and I started having sex. And when I told Mom I thought I was pregnant, she looked even more shocked than Luke had. "You think you're WHAT?"

Then she just blew up. "I don't believe this! After all we've talked about, you go and screw around with your boyfriend without even using a condom? You wanted to have sex with Luke so bad you couldn't be bothered to— where was your brain, Lucy?"

I tried to get a word in. Mom barreled right over me. "I thought I could trust you! All these years of making sure I was here for you! When I finally think you're old enough to leave home alone for a few hours, what do you do? You raid the liquor cabinet and get yourself pregnant!"

Mom barely stopped to take a breath. "Let's get one thing straight, Lucy. You've seen my life. You should know how hard it is to raise a baby when you're seventeen. I did it once. Not again!"

And she went into her bedroom and slammed the door.

I was completely stunned. Mom never yells at me like this. Even when she's mad, she always listens. It doesn't matter how stupid I've been or what kind of mess I've gotten into. Her favorite line is always, "We can work this out."

But not this time. This time even my own mother slammed the door on me. First Luke and now Mom. I felt totally alone.

CHAPTER 12

The first thing I saw when I woke up Sunday morning was Mom's face. She was sitting on the floor next to my bed. She looked as if she hadn't slept all night.

"Hey," she said softly, "I am so, so sorry for last night, Lucy. I don't have any excuse. I was just so shocked. I fail as a mom."

I started to cry. Mom crawled in bed with me. "Shhhh," she said, stroking my hair. "It's okay, baby. You're okay. We'll work this out."

Mom rubbed my back while she talked. "I came into your room the minute I calmed down last night. I was so ashamed of myself. I sounded just like *my* mother. I wanted to say sorry, but you were sound asleep. So I just stayed here, in case you woke up."

Mom kept talking and rubbing until I stopped sniffling. "Now hop in the shower," she said briskly. "I'll make breakfast."

I felt better after a hot shower. Mom had poached eggs and tea all ready. It actually tasted good. I talked and talked while I ate.

"And now Luke won't even talk to me," I finished sadly. "I think he hates me."

"Oh, I doubt that," Mom said. "But he's scared. He doesn't want anything to do with having a baby. He wants to run away."

"So do I!" I wailed.

Now Mom sounded sad too. "I'm sure you do, Lucy. But you can't. That's the reality. Guys can run away from pregnancy. Girls can't." She hesitated. "I wouldn't count on Luke too much from here on out."

"No!" I protested. "You're wrong. Luke loves me!"

Mom didn't seem to hear. "We'll have to talk to Luke's parents," she said. "I'm not going to let you go through what I did. Luke's family has enough money. He can help support the baby." She sighed. "We'll have to talk to a lawyer, I guess."

I felt a little panicky. Mom was talking about my life like I didn't even have a say!

Luke didn't answer my phone calls all day. When I went to school on Monday, he seemed to be avoiding me. I didn't see him at lunch. He got on the baseball bus after school without even saying good-bye.

It was that way all week. I knew Luke was really busy. Normally we'd be making plans to celebrate after the playoff game next week. Now he wouldn't even answer my text messages. I didn't even know if he wanted me to come to the game!

Things weren't perfect at home either. Mom was being really nice to me. But she acted as if Luke wasn't in the picture at all.

She had me take the home pregnancy test again, just to be sure. When it still showed up positive, she made a doctor's appointment for me.

"Four o'clock next Monday," she said. "I'm taking the afternoon off. I'll pick you up right after school."

"But I want Luke to come with me!" I protested. "It's our baby! He should be there."

Mom just looked at me. "Is that what he wants?"

I couldn't say. Luke still wasn't answering my calls or texts.

By the end of the week I was resigned. Mom was right. Luke might not hate me. But he didn't want anything to do with me now that I was pregnant.

I was sad and tired when Mom dropped me off at the studio Saturday morning. It was a crazy day. All the little kids seemed cranky and out of sorts.

Even cute Tierney Murphy was misbehaving. She didn't want to wear the leotard her mom brought. "I said the pink one!" she wailed. She flung the black one away from her and managed to hit her little brother.

TJ howled. Mrs. Murphy sat cross-legged on the floor. She took Tierney on one knee and TJ on the other. She nuzzled TJ's red, tearful face as she slipped off Tierney's T-shirt and jeans. When Tierney wiggled in protest, Mrs. Murphy tickled her tummy.

Tierney giggled. Mrs. Murphy pulled on the black leotard with one quick motion. She stood up and balanced TJ on her hip. When she bent over to straighten Tierney's shoulder strap, TJ gave a huge burp and spat up all over his sister.

Both kids started wailing again. Mrs. Murphy raised her eyebrows at me. "It's been like this all day," she said. "It never ends." Then she patiently hushed TJ and steered Tierney toward the bathroom to mop up.

Is this what being a mother is like? Always having to be patient and nice and take care of someone else's problems? It suddenly hit me that I wouldn't just be having a baby. I'd be having a baby and a three-year-old and a ten-year-old and a seventeen-year-old. *Once you're a mother, you're a mother for life. It never ends.*

I tried to talk to Cate and Trez about how weird and scary everything was after class, but they didn't really get it. Cate was still stuck on having a baby shower. Trez had news about Luke.

"Lonzo says Luke's really focused on baseball now. The Austin scout is supposed to be at the playoff game tomorrow. They think he's going to make the scholarship offer then."

This just made me sadder. Luke hadn't told me any of this. "Luke still isn't talking to me," I said. "I guess I won't be going to the game."

"Oh, c'mon," Cate said, "it'll be fun. The shortstop from Eastside is supposed to be really hot. A girl in my church knows him."

"I don't think Lucy's interested in hot guys right now," Trez said. She gave me a concerned look. "How are you feeling these days, anyhow? Still sick?"

I shrugged. "Better, I guess. At least I'm not fainting anymore."

Trez hesitated. "Have you thought any more about—you know, an abortion?"

I shook my head. "I think about stuff all the time. But I don't know if I could do it. I mean, I still believe women should be able to have abortions. But when I think about me, right now . . ." I didn't know how to finish. "It's my *baby*. I don't even know whether it's a he or a she, but I already think of her as my daughter."

"What does Luke say?" Trez asked.

I shrugged. "How would I know? He's not talking to me."

Trez hugged me while I tried not to cry.

Cate finished packing her dance bag. "So, then, when are you going to tell Toni?" she asked. "I mean, about not dancing in the show?"

I was startled. Not dance in the show? Of course I was going to dance in the show! I had a solo! Then I really thought about it. The show was over a month away. I had no idea what my body would be like in a month. Would I still be throwing up? Would I be able to stretch and bend and keep my balance as I moved across the floor? Would I even fit into a dance leotard?

I remembered my favorite quote. "To dance is to be out of yourself. Larger, more beautiful, more powerful." As a pregnant dancer, I'd be larger, that's for sure.

CHAPTER 13

I was only half listening to Cate and Trez as we walked to Cate's car after class. So I didn't really notice when they both fell silent. Trez nudged me.

I looked up. Luke was standing there.

"Hi," he said awkwardly. He nodded to Cate and Trez. "I thought I could give you a ride. If that's okay."

I didn't know what to say. I'd pretty much given up on Luke by now. Seeing him here made me feel confused. I hated how he'd been acting. But he was still Luke. And in spite of everything, I still loved him.

"I guess so," I said cautiously. I looked at Cate and Trez. "See you tomorrow?"

Luke didn't start the car right away. He just sat there staring straight ahead. Then he reached over and took my hand. "I've missed you, Lucy," he said.

I was suddenly really mad. I snatched my hand away. "Missed *me*? Or missed having sex with me?"

He flinched. "I don't blame you for being mad, Lucy," he said. "I've done everything wrong. I just—I don't know. I panicked. I was stupid. I'm sorry."

I didn't answer. Luke waited. Then he went on. "I've been thinking about you all week, Lucy. I don't care if you're pregnant. I mean, I do care. I care a lot. I care about YOU a lot. I miss you all the time. I don't want to break up because you're having a baby. Our baby."

I breathed a long, shaky sigh of relief. This was more like the Luke I knew. I wasn't sure where we'd go from here. But at least for now, Luke was back.

Slowly, carefully, we started talking to each other. I told Luke about Mom's blowup. "I've never seen her so mad. But she's calmed down now."

"I bet she hates me," Luke said.

"No," I said, "she just doesn't believe you'll stick around." Then I had a thought. "Why? Do your parents hate me?"

"My dad's pretty mad," Luke said honestly. "He thinks—I think he thinks you got pregnant on purpose."

"On purpose!" I was shocked. "Why would I do that?"

Luke looked embarrassed. "You know— to trap me. To keep me here with you in Houston, instead of going to Austin."

Now I was mad again. "Is that what you told him? That I just wanted to make you stay here with me?"

"No! Nothing like that! But you know—all that stuff you said about cheerleaders and coed dorms. And the vodka and stuff."

"You told your dad all that?"

"He asked me!" Luke looked flustered. "I didn't know what to say!"

I was more sad now than mad. "What about your mom? Does she hate me too?"

Luke smiled for the first time. "No. My mom told my dad it takes two to tango. She said if I didn't know enough to use protection, it was my own damn fault."

I smiled a little, too. "It's so weird, isn't it? I mean, us having a baby."

Luke nodded. "You should hear my parents. They're really upset, but they're already talking about their grandchild. I think my mom will help you take care of it."

I wasn't sure I'd heard Luke right. "Your mom will help *me* take care of it?" I repeated, very slowly.

"Yeah, you know. When I'm in Austin. I think my mom will help you and your mom babysit and all."

I hesitated. I didn't want to make Luke mad when we were just starting to talk again. But I'd had a lot of time to think this past week. I couldn't play games with him. I had to be honest. I plunged right in.

"In the first place, Luke, the baby isn't an 'it.' She's a he or a she, a *person*. In the second place, she's not just *my* baby to take care of. She's *our* baby—yours and mine. In the third place, your mom doesn't get to say what kind of help we need."

Luke looked really surprised. "My mom was just trying to be nice, Lucy!"

I sighed. "I know, Luke. My mom's trying to be nice too. But we're the ones who have to make the decisions about this baby. Because she's ours. We're her mother and father. We have to take care of her ourselves."

"But I'll be in Austin next year!" Luke said. "I don't know how you think I can babysit when I'll be taking a full course load and playing baseball!"

"It's not babysitting when it's your own baby!"

"I'm not ready to be a father, Lucy!"

"And you think I'm ready to be a mother?" I snapped.

We both sat there in an angry silence. I felt miserable again. "I don't want us to be mad, Luke," I said slowly. "I just think we should try to figure things out ourselves. We need to be talking to each other. Not just listening to our parents."

"But they're our parents, Lucy! They might be mad, but they love us. They want what's best for us."

I smiled a little. "Is that what your mom said? Because it's what mine said. But that's just what I mean, Luke. They're our parents. They love us and want what's best for us. Well, we're our baby's parents. We have to love her and do what's best for her."

I hesitated. I wanted Luke to know everything I'd been thinking.

"I thought about having an abortion," I said steadily. "It's almost the first thing I thought about."

Luke looked down at his hands. "You still could," he said in a low voice. "Have an abortion, I mean. It could fix everything."

I shook my head. "No," I said sadly. "I don't think so. I mean—it's just—she's too real to me already."

Luke sighed. "If that's the way you feel, that's the way it'll be. I told you I've been thinking a lot this week too, Lucy. I'm not going to run away anymore—whatever you decide is what we'll do. So I guess we're back to being good parents and raising our baby ourselves."

"Maybe not," I answered slowly. I told Luke about the list of four options I'd thought of that long, sad night after I told him I was pregnant. "I really don't think I can have an abortion," I said. "And I know I can't pretend this never happened. So we have two choices left. We can try to raise our baby ourselves. Or we can let another mom and dad raise her."

I spoke so low, Luke had to lean over to hear me. "What are you saying, Lucy?" he asked incredulously. "Are you saying we should give our baby away? Let some strangers adopt him?"

I felt a tear roll down my cheek. "I don't know, Luke," I said. "Maybe. Maybe that's the best way we can be good parents. By loving our baby enough to let someone else take care of her. Maybe we shouldn't make our baby grow up with a mom and dad who aren't ready to be parents. Maybe we should love our baby enough to let her have better parents. A mom and dad who really, truly want her."

Luke was quiet for a long, long time. Then he reached over and took my hand. This time I let him. We sat there, just holding hands.

"This is too hard," Luke said finally. "It's just too damn hard."

CHAPTER 14

I woke up on Sunday feeling better than I had in weeks. Luke and I hadn't really solved anything. But at least we were talking. And he was picking me up for the playoff game this afternoon.

"Plus," I told Mom, "Luke says he wants to come to the doctor's appointment with me tomorrow."

"And after the baby is born?" she asked. "Is Luke going to give up Austin to stay here and be a father?"

I shook my head. "I don't know, Mom. Neither of us knows. We've just started talking." I took a deep breath. "We're talking about a lot of things. I want to talk to you too. About our options. About adoption."

Mom looked as if I'd slapped her. "Adoption? You mean, give your baby to someone else? But Lucy—this is your child! Your flesh and blood!"

"We haven't decided anything, Mom," I said. "We're just thinking about it."

Mom took a deep breath. "Think about this, Lucy. Sure, it's hard to imagine your whole life changing right now—trust me, I've been there, I know. But what *you* don't know, what you can't imagine, is how much you'd miss your baby the rest of your life."

Mom took my face in her hands. "Keeping you is the hardest thing and the best thing I ever did. I've never regretted having you for one single second!"

I felt a little desperate. "But I'm not you, Mom! I don't think I can do what you did! I'm not strong enough to be a good mother to my baby. I want her to have everything I can't give her."

Mom looked sad now, not mad. "All the things I couldn't give you."

"No!" I said fiercely. "You gave me everything. But that's what I mean. Babies take everything! I don't think I can give up so much of my life! I don't think I can be a good mom like you."

Mom didn't say anything for a long minute. Then she put her arms around me and rocked me, standing right there in the kitchen. "There are all kinds of ways of being a good mother," she said. She laughed a little shakily. "You're already thinking about what's best for your baby. I guess that's all any of us moms can ever do."

I thought about being good parents while I watched Luke's playoff game. He was terrific as ever. Better, even. He played maybe the best game of his life. I didn't want Luke to give up baseball. I didn't want him to give up college. I didn't want to give up dance or college either. I didn't know what to do.

Trez got to the game late. "Lonzo and I are taking another break," she announced when she joined me and Cate on the first-base line. "I'm not ready to go to the next step, and he definitely is."

Cate looked interested. "You mean sex?" she asked. "Maybe I should talk to Lonzo!"

Trez rolled her eyes. "You're impossible. Let's talk about something else!"

Cate shrugged agreeably. "Like Lucy's baby shower? I was thinking maybe we should have it in your backyard, Trez. You have that nice deck. Yellow and green would be a good color scheme for summer. It could work for either a boy or a girl."

I let their conversation roll over me. I hadn't said anything to Cate and Trez about adoption. I didn't want to, not until Luke and I had talked more.

Luke found me right after the game. He looked excited. He gave me a huge hug and kiss, just like the old days. "I got the scholarship, Lucy! Full ride! The scout just told us! We're going to sign the papers tomorrow, right after school!"

I hugged Luke back. "That's so wonderful! I'm so happy for you!" Then I remembered. "But I thought—"

Luke avoided my eyes. "I'm not forgetting the baby. I know we still have a lot to figure out. But I'm not giving up this scholarship!"

I shook my head. "I don't want you to. But that's not what I mean. Tomorrow afternoon is my doctor's appointment. I thought you wanted to go with me . . ."

My voice trailed off as I noticed Luke's mom and dad coming up behind him.

"Everything all right here?" asked Luke's dad.

"It's just—" I began, "my first pregnancy appointment. It's tomorrow right after school. Luke said he wanted to go with me."

Luke's parents exchanged glances. "Those doctor's appointments are really more for moms-to-be," Mrs. Gilman said smoothly. "And the meeting with the Austin representative has already been set up."

Mrs. Gilman smiled at me. "I know we haven't talked yet, Lucy. And we have a lot to talk about, with this grandbaby coming along. But right now Luke needs to concentrate on Austin. Next week, we could all get together—you, your mom, us." She brightened. "We'll touch base about your appointment, and . . ."

I felt that hopeless sinking feeling again. Luke still wouldn't meet my eyes. I didn't see how I could fight both him and his parents. It might be our baby, but it was my responsibility.

"Sure," I said, "fine, see you later then."

I turned to leave. If I hurried, I could still catch a ride home with Cate.

"Wait," said Luke. He caught my hand and pulled me back. He turned to face his parents.

"Mom, Dad, I know this scholarship means a lot to you. It means a lot to me and Lucy too. But I can sign those papers any time. Tomorrow I'm going with Lucy to her doctor's appointment."

Luke's dad started to protest. Luke cut him off. "Austin can wait a day or two, Dad. You and Mom raised me to be responsible and to do the right thing. Well, Lucy's pregnant and I'm responsible. Tomorrow I'm taking Lucy to the doctor, and right now I'm taking her home. I'll see you back at the house in a little while."

Then Luke put his arm around me and steered me firmly toward his car.

CHAPTER 15

Mom dropped me off at school as usual on Monday.

"See you this afternoon at the doctor's," she said. "Luke's still giving you a ride?"

I nodded. "I'll see you at four." I tried to smile, but it came out pretty crooked. "I'm scared."

Mom reached over the seat to hug me. "You'd be nuts not to be scared," she said. "I'll be right there with you," she added. "And so will Luke."

I was nervous all day. By the time the afternoon bell rang, I was about ready to jump out of my skin.

Cate and Trez walked me out to Luke's car. "Call me when you're done," Trez said. "Let me know if you want me to stop by tonight."

"Find out if it's a boy or a girl!" Cate added. "I want to pick colors for the shower!"

I made another snap decision. "No shower, Cate," I said firmly. "I'm pregnant. I'm having a baby. After that, I don't know what's going to happen."

Cate looked confused. "What do you mean? After that you'll need all the shower stuff for your baby. You don't even have any diapers!"

"I may not need diapers," I said slowly.

Trez was watching me closely. "Adoption?" she said softly. "I wondered if you were thinking of that."

I nodded. "Luke and I don't know what we're doing," I told them both. "We have a lot to think about. But I'll let you guys know when I know. I don't think I can do this without you!"

Trez hugged me hard. "We'll always be here for you!" she said. She nudged Cate. "Right?"

Cate still looked a little confused. "Well, of course! But I don't understand . . ."

Trez steered Cate toward her car. "I'll explain on the way to dance," she said. "Good luck, Lucy!"

Luke and I got to the doctor's office early. We walked around the little park across the street while we waited for Mom.

"All this time, and I haven't even asked you how you feel," Luke said. "Are you okay?"

"Except for wanting to throw up and having to pee all the time, you mean?" I said. "I'm okay. I definitely feel different though."

"You look different," he said, sort of shy. "Glowy, maybe. I like it. But I'm sorry about the throwing up."

I laughed. "Mom says it'll get better in a few weeks." Then I had a question for Luke. "How come you decided to come with me today instead of meeting with the Austin scout?"

Luke took my hand. "I remembered something your mom said once, when we were first going out. It was about your dad. Your mom said he wasn't a bad guy, he just wasn't ready to be a father."

I nodded. That's what Mom always says.

"But I've been thinking, Lucy," Luke said seriously. "I don't want to hurt your feelings or anything, but your dad WAS a bad guy! He left your mom! He left YOU. I don't want to be that kind of a guy. I don't want you to have to tell our baby why I didn't stick around."

"But you're not ready to be a father either," I said.

"And you're not ready to be a mother."

We walked around without talking for a while. It was a nice afternoon. The play area in the little park was filled with kids and their parents. I watched a toddler wobble across the grass, laughing as her mom chased after her. Could I really give up my baby for adoption?

"My mom raised me by herself," I said, thinking out loud. "It wasn't easy, but she did it. I could probably do the same thing."

Luke nodded. He was watching two little boys kicking a soccer ball. "Or I could give up Austin and raise the baby with you," he said. "We could both find jobs. We could take turns staying home. Take a few classes at the community college. Maybe in a few years we could even go to the university. It would take longer, and I'd lose my scholarship, but eventually we could get our degrees. I could still be a coach. You could still be a teacher."

"But I don't want you to give up your scholarship!" I said. "And—I don't want to give up high school, and dance, and studying Spanish in college. Is that selfish? Or is it more selfish to keep our baby just because she's ours? Even if we can't give her the kind of life we want her to have?"

We watched the kids playing. "I don't even know my baby yet," I said sadly. "But I already love her. I already know that giving her up for adoption would be the hardest thing I'd ever have to do."

"I think my parents would be mad about adoption," Luke said. "I mean, they're not happy you're pregnant, but they're already calling the baby their grandbaby."

I nodded. "My mom too."

"But like you said before, this is OUR baby," Luke said. "He's not our parents' baby. We have to be the ones to decide what's best for him. What's best for all of us."

"I can't stand the thought of never knowing my baby. What if I had never known my mom?" I cried. "But I want our baby to have a real family! I want her to have a mom and dad who want her and love her and know how to take care of her and protect her!"

I burst into tears. Luke held me for a long, long moment.

"There aren't going to be any easy answers, are there?" he asked, finally.

I shook my head, sniffing. "Not anymore." I thought about everything that had happened these past weeks. "But at least—at least now we're figuring things out together."

We watched Mom's car pull up in the doctor's parking lot. She got out and waved.

"I guess it's time," Luke said.

We started walking across the park. "Mom says we'll probably hear the baby's heartbeat today," I said.

I shivered. Our baby was real. She had a heartbeat. Soon I'd be able to feel her moving around inside me. Then she'd be born, and she'd grow, and some nice afternoon someone would bring her to play in a park just like this one. Would that someone be me?

"Are you ready?" asked Luke. He took my hand and held it firmly.

I took a deep breath. Getting pregnant had never been part of my plan. But life happens, and now here I was. Here *we* were, I mentally corrected myself.

Because I wasn't in this alone anymore. From now on, whatever happened, it would be because Luke and I decided together what was best for our baby.

"Yes," I said. "No. I don't know. Let's go."

About the Author

Charnan Simon lives in Seattle, Washington, and has written more than one hundred books for young readers. Her two daughters are mostly grown up, and she misses having teenagers running in and out of the house.

SOUTHSIDE HIGH

ARE YOU A SURVIVOR?

check out All the books in the

SURVIVING SOUTH SIDE

collection.

Bad Deal

Fish hates having to take ADHD meds. They help him concentrate but also make him feel weird. So when a cute girl needs a boost to study for tests, Fish offers her one of his pills. Soon more kids want pills, and Fish likes the profits. To keep from running out, Fish finds a doctor who sells phony prescriptions. But suddenly the doctor is arrested. Fish realizes he needs to tell the truth. But will that cost him his friends?

Recruited

Kadeem is a star quarterback for Southside High. He is thrilled when college scouts seek him out. One recruiter even introduces him to a college cheerleader and gives him money to have a good time. But then officials start to investigate illegal recruiting. Will Kadeem decide to help their investigation, even though it means the end of the good times? What will it do to his chances of playing in college?

Benito Runs

Benito's father had been in Iraq for over a year. When he returns, Benito's family life is not the same. Dad suffers from PTSD—post-traumatic stress disorder—and yells constantly. Benito can't handle seeing his dad so crazy, so he decides to run away. Will Benny find a new life? Or will he learn how to deal with his dad—through good times and bad?

PLAN B

Lucy has her life planned: she'll graduate and join her boyfriend at college in Austin. She'll become a Spanish teacher and of course they'll get married. So there's no reason to wait, right? They try to be careful, but Lucy gets pregnant. Lucy's plan is gone. How will she make the most difficult decision of her life?

BEATEN

Keah's a cheerleader and Ty's a football star, so they seem like the perfect couple. But when they have their first fight, Ty is beginning to scare Keah with his anger. Then after losing a game, Ty goes ballistic and hits Keah repeatedly. Ty is arrested for assault, but Keah still secretly meets up with Ty. How can Keah be with someone she's afraid of? What's worse—flinching every time your boyfriend gets angry, or being alone?

Shattered Star

Cassie is the best singer at Southside and dreams of being famous. She skips school to try out for a national talent competition. But her hopes sink when she sees the line. Then a talent agent shows up, and Cassie is flattered to hear she has "the look" he wants. Soon she is lying and missing rehearsal to meet with him. And he's asking her for more each time. How far will Cassie go for her shot at fame?

THE PROTECTORS

Luke's life has never been "normal." How could it be, with
his mother holding séances and his stepfather working as a
mortician? But living in a funeral home never bothered Luke
until the night of his mom's accident.

Sounds of screaming now shatter Luke's dreams. And his
stepfather is acting even stranger. When bodies in the funeral
home start delivering messages, Luke is certain that he's nuts. As
he tries to solve his mother's death, Luke discovers a secret more
horrifying than any nightmare.

SKIN

It looks like a pizza exploded on Nick Barry's face. But bad skin
is the least of his problems. His bones feel like living ice. A
strange rash—like scratches—seems to be some sort of ancient
code. And then there's the anger . . .

Something evil is living under Nick's skin. Where did it
come from? What does it want? With the help of a dead kid's
diary, a nun, and a local professor, Nick slowly finds out what's
wrong with him. But there's still one question that Nick must
face alone: how do you destroy an evil that's *inside* you?

THAW

A July storm caused a major power outage in Bridgewater. Now a research project at the Institute for Cryogenic Experimentation has been ruined, and the thawed-out bodies of twenty-seven federal inmates are missing.

At first, Dani didn't think much of the news. But after her best friend Jake disappears, a mysterious visitor connects the dots for Dani. Jake has been taken in by a cult. To get him back, Dani must enter a dangerous, alternate reality where a defrosted cult leader is beginning to act like some kind of god.

UNTHINKABLE

Omar Phillips is Bridgewater High's favorite teen author. His fans can't wait for his next horror story. But lately Omar's imagination has turned against him. Horrifying visions of death and destruction haunt him. The only way to stop the visions is to write them down. Until they start coming true . . .

Enter Sophie Minax, the mysterious girl who's been following Omar at school. "I'm one of you," Sophie says. She tells Omar how to end the visions—but the only thing worse than Sophie's cure may be what happens if he ignores it.

THE CLUB

The club started innocently enough. Bored after school, Josh and his friends decided to try out an old board game. Called "Black Magic," it promised players good fortune at the expense of those who have wronged them.

But when the club members' luck starts skyrocketing—and horror befalls their enemies—the game stops being a joke. How can they stop what they've unleashed? Answers lie in an old diary—but ending the game may be deadlier than any curse.

MESSAGES FROM BEYOND

Some guy named Ethan has been texting Cassie. He seems to know all about her—but she can't place him. He's not in the yearbook either. Cassie thinks one of her friends is punking her. But she can't ignore the strange coincidences—like how Ethan looks just like the guy in her nightmares.

Cassie's search for Ethan leads her to a shocking discovery—and a struggle for her life. Will Cassie be able to break free from her mysterious stalker?